KIRK DODSON

Never Have I Ever

For the little ones who dream.

Never have I ever swam with a whale.

But I will !

Never have I ever hang glided.

Never have I ever hugged a giant tortoise.

Never have I ever road in a hot air balloon.

Never have I ever marched with penguins.

But I will !

Never have I ever rode in a submarine.

Never have I ever bathed an elephant.

Never have I ever climbed to the top of an apple tree.

Never have I ever hung
out with a sloth.

Never have I ever jumped from the highest diving board.

But I will !

Never have I ever rode a camel.

But I will !

Never have I ever painted a masterpiece.

Never have I ever walked on the moon.

Create your own things to do !

Never have I ever

Draw the thing you want to do !

Create your own things to do !

Never have I ever

Draw the thing you want to do !

Create your own things to do !

Never have I ever

Draw the thing you want to do !

Create your own things to do !

Never have I ever

Draw the thing you want to do !

Kirk Dodson was born thousands of years ago, on top of a magical mountain in 1976. He spent his youth singing karaoke with dragons and playing dodgeball with elves. When Kirk finally went to college, he earned his bachelor's degree in sculpture from the Memphis College of Arts. Kirk spent many years creating art for creatures such as gnomes, goblins, and politicians. One day Kirk found a wild hair under a rock, and decided to start writing children's books. It should be noted, that Kirk has a GINORMOUS imagination, and should not be taken seriously!

www.ingramcontent.com/pod-product-compliance
Lightning Source LLC
Chambersburg PA
CBHW041002170626
46815CB00002B/116